THE MAGICAL CHRISTMAS BOOK

GRACE FOSTER

Dedicated to.
my husband, Patrick
and our beautiful
daughter, Coco.

This book belongs to

Grace and Orla
were so
excited.

It was nearly
Christmas.

DECEMBER
1 2 3 4 5 6
8 9 10 13
7 18
22
25

Twin sisters, Grace
and Orla, had
already posted their
letters to Santa.

SANTA CLAUS
NORTH POLE

'How do you
think the letter
gets to Santa?'
Grace asked Orla.

POST

'it must be by magic'
Orla said.

‘I am so excited,’
Orla says to Grace.
‘Me too,’
Grace replies.
‘I can’t wait until Christmas.’

In the morning
the girls woke up
and guess what
was at the
bottom of their bed?

... their favourite
Christmas book!

'How does the book
get here, every year?'
Grace asked Orla.
'By magic, of
course,' Orla said.

‘I love this story.
It’s the best Christmas book ever,’
Grace says happily.

'What is the big deal about this book
and Christmas?'
their sister, Linda, asked.

The girls had
great fun all day
building a Snowman.

The girls read
their favourite story
once more, before
going up to bed.

At night-time,
the girls tip-toed
downstairs to the
sitting room.

scan Me

They played their
favourite song
and danced.

'Girls,' Mam called.
'It's bedtime.'

The girls laugh
excitedly and return
to their bedroom.

Every night
before Christmas Eve,
the girls take turns reading
the Christmas book
to each other.

'I can't wait until Santa comes,'
Orla said, as the girls hung
up their stockings.

G
O

They read their Christmas book
for the last time
that year.

'I am sad
the book will magically
disappear for another year,'
said Orla.

'See you next year,' Grace said,
placing the book on the end
of her bed.

'Let's look out
the window,' Grace said.
'We might even see
Santa in the sky?'

‘It’s our book!’
Grace points.

Amazed, the girls
watched as a white
owl carried their book
high into the sky.

In a flash of light,
both the owl and the
book disappeared.

That night their
dreams were about Santa
and his elves,
in the North Pole.

In the morning,
the girls
excitedly ran downstairs
to see if Santa
had arrived.

The girls were so
happy.
SANTA
had arrived!!!

'Look at all the
presents under
the tree, Grace said.
'Looks like Santa
got our letter, Orla replied.

'That was a really
fun day,
Grace said.
'I love all my presents.

'Yes, me too,
Orla replied.
'But I can't wait to see our
Christmas book again next year.

eales
lores
Holly
Tolly
Stores
Big
Holly
Holiay
Cletems
Ga

Merry Christmas,
everyone!

Page 37. Song 'Cotton Eye Joe' by Rednex

BUTTERFLY BOOKS
PUBLISHERS
nicolakearnswriting.com

www.ingramcontent.com/pod-product-compliance
Lightning Source LLC
Chambersburg PA
CBHW041410300726
48978CB00002B/43